CLIT CHRONICLES

CATHRYN MARIE

http://overtheedgebooks.com/

Clit Chronicles written by Cathryn Marie
Photography & Cover design by Bella Clarke
www.shotbybella.com

clit chronicles

Cathryn Marie

Clit Chronicles
Table Of Contents

The Clit Chronicles were birthed in 2006 as a pass time hobby and became reading material for my AOL Friends on MySpace. Producing material that was never proof read and/or edited, I created stories based upon stories and/or moments that others shared with me - being a loyal AOL chat room junkie, getting stories became second nature. From an intimate circle to growing fans, Clit Chronicles took over a life of its own as Friends shared with their Friends and so on and so on.

What's taken so long for me to finally produce this project? I just simply didn't feel encouraged by the sex - I didn't own it. Fears of being labeled or people reading the stories and thinking they are personal experiences, worried I'd embarrass my Family - I just didn't want this project to be more than what it was. After talking to my Dad & me telling him about my content, getting his support empowered me to finally own my work! Owning my sex and knowing that what I write about doesn't reflect who I am as a person and knowing that it's just sex!

My writings are not personal experiences - in great detail ... You will not read one story that is a reflection of my life.

Supporters along the way include Actor Poncho Hodges, Hakimu Davidson, Poet Perry "Vision" Divirgilio, "Cooper", Delano Washington, Robert "RL" Huggar of R & B Group NEXT and my great support system throughout the GREAT city of Houston, Texas... My supportive "fan club" from MySpace, I only pray that you find this book. I thank you all, as if it weren't for you, I wouldn't have produced as much writing as I did.

Inspiration along the way is credited to incredible Enitan Bereola and to Ms. Beverly Thomas for the unconditional love; I thank you!.

2014 the year of the Clit Chronicles... Special thanks to the publishing companies that denied my graphic content and to Paul Stewart at Over the Edge for encouraging me to not change anything...

"Once people understand that your sexual desires do not define who you are as a person, the world will be a better place" ...
- CathrynMarie

Clit Chronicles: Unspoken Chemistry

There was nothing to talk about. There wasn't even time to set the mood with music. We both knew what we desired, leaving time only for us to claw one another's clothing off. The fire shared between the two of us was met with each sexually stimulated kiss. His full lips overlapping my bottom lip. His tongue wandering through my lips, meeting up with my tongue allotting our saliva together form a bond of the souls meeting with our mouths.

Laying me on the edge of the bed, he removed my volleyball shorts, which were worn with no under garments. Before his lips met my pussy, his breathe was felt on my clit as he whispered, "What a pretty pussy!" Without further hesitation, Anthony wrapped his left arm around my right thigh, bringing his left hand around my waist down to my clit. With his index and middle fingers, he pressed upon my vagina, allowing the lips around it to meet his face – that's when he spit on it. He knows the extent of how much I love when he does that, so he spit on her again. With the same affection he shared when our tongues danced, he conveyed the same energy while sucking on my clit. With my body squirming and trembling from the pleasure coming from between my legs, Anthony took it a step further and slid his right index finger into my opening. The constant stimulation from his mouth kissing my pussy and his finger contributing to my natural juices overflowing out of the hole he was focused on. My body squirming quickly turned into air thrusts and grinding motions towards his mouth, probing him to once again spit on my love box.

I wanted to kiss him. I wanted to taste myself on his lips. Sitting in an upright position, leaving him to rise up, I cuffed the bottom of his chin with my right hand and kissed him passionately. Sticking my tongue out and licking all over his lips, he caught the drift of what I was doing and whispered for me to continue to lick my juices off of his lips. Spying a missed drop in the corner of his mouth, I pressed my lips against his, slid my tongue in his mouth, pulled away just a bit and embarked on my wetness on the side of his mouth. Like any man with a mission, my touching moment was broken up by him finding his way back between my legs to continue his feast until I reached my peak.

Feeling satisfied and eager to please him, using my right hand, I lifted his head from between my legs, took his left hand in mine and guided for him to stand up. Standing in front of me with his boxers on, I proceeded to pull down the material standing between me and his glorified package that I knew awaited me. With my palms placed on his thighs, I opened my mouth wide and welcomed his dick to the back of my throat. He proceeded to grip the back of my head with his hands, pushing his dick deeper within my opening. Easing up a bit, his dick laid on my tongue in the middle of my mouth where I then clinched my jaws together and began sucking his dick midway, all the way to his tip. Each time his tip met my lips, I would improve the grip formed with by my lips; squeezing and sucking on his mushroom tighter. Allowing my mouth to fill with more saliva as I maintained my position of pleasing him orally, I would swallow his whole dick in an effort to make myself gag on his manhood. With my eyes watering from taking all of that force in the back of my mouth, I looked up at him which prompted him to encourage me not to stop by again gripping the back of my head, this time allowing his fingers to get tangled in my hair as he tugged on it.

Pulling his dick out of my mouth, he motioned for me to get on all fours with my rear end facing him. Complying with his request and before getting comfortable in position, I felt his let palm grip my left butt cheek and his tongue sucking on my lips from the back. Getting lost in the feeling of satisfaction was quickly interrupted when I felt myself being elevated. Anthony was surely introducing me to something new, as he bent his knees, wrapped his forearms around my thighs from the back, pulled me towards his shoulders and wrapped my legs around his neck, before once again getting lost and devouring my pussy with his mouth. Completely enjoying what was taking place, I realized that I was upside in his arms with my legs around his neck, with his penis staring right in my face – I returned the favor and began giving him head while in a headstand position. Gripping the back of his thighs made easy for me to push his dick deep into my mouth as I sucked his dick up side down. The sensation coming from his end was far too much too handle after another seven minutes or so of this experience – perhaps it was the new position but I found myself sliding down and demanding he service me with his dick.

Knowing when to be submissive and listen to me, Anthony reached for a condom, slid it on and found his way to my opening as I lay on my back to greet him with my warm vagina. Shoving his dick deep inside of me, I cannot recall the last time I felt so much passion – it was as if his energy was being pushed off on to me. Uttering how much I missed feeling his dick inside of me, only seemed to give him super-hero powers and when I told him that my pussy belonged to him, his strong thrusts stopped briefly only for him to switch positions and have me doggy-style, where he continued to give me long strokes of love. Sliding his left index finger in my rear, while giving me his dick, I would back my ass up towards him in an effort for his finger to get deeper in my exit hole. Taking his dick out and slapping it on my ass, I continued to back my ass up towards him, hoping he caught on that I wanted to feel his dick in my ass. Forcefully pushing his penis back inside my vagina, he removed his finger for my ass and proceeded to spit on my rear opening, when he then slid his index and middle finger into the now wet opening.

The passion that ensues within two people whom which share an increased of sexual attraction, admiration and appreciation is what we were experiencing for the next fifteen minutes. He continued to fuck me with great passion from the back, while I maintain my position on all fours, never sliding down or running away – his dick fits my pussy so well, there was no need to run. When he told me he was coming, I clinched my walls around his dick to where it was a tight grip that he felt – somewhat like when I sucked the tip of his dick. His moans echoed throughout the apartment; music to my ears yet discomfort for my neighbors. Anthony always knows how to make each experience different – each time we have sex, it's nothing like the last time. Which is why words are never spoken once the mood is set – only passion speaks and boy does it speak volumes...

As long as we know that we want to be together, we will be fine; we're a work in progress.

Clit Chronicles: No Longer A Virgin

Freshmen year, the glory days of every 14 year-old student, the year of decision making; grown enough to stand up for yourself and ask your parents to let you hang out, yet too young for them to actually say yes. Not only are new friendships and relationships built during the first year of High School but the outline of the course and path one is headed starts the first year of High School; the grades you start off with are probably the grades you'll leave with, not to mention the people you associate with and their influence on you as a person will now set the stage of how you will end that first year. I entered as a student with A's and B's, a virgin, kept my association with people to a minimum and boy friendless. By the end of 12th grade year – wait, I didn't make it that far – I was pregnant, a high school dropout and had a boy friend who was 10 years my senior.

Sex – everyone was having it, but my being a victim of vaginal molestation at a young age, I had no interest in it. The only girl within a 3 block range, in any direction of my neighborhood, the male species preyed on me like a dog to a steak. I was proportioned nicely; 5'5, 119, 36/26/36 and the older men loved it. Associating with anyone 18 years of age was out of the question for me. When I met Theo, I know I should have walked away – he was too old for me – but I took his number and later used it.

The day I met Leon, I was walking my 15 or so block walk home from school with my best friend, Corina. Just returning from a school field trip at the ice skating rink, we shared laughs and teenage conversation. Leon was in a Red two-door, Ford Escort when he passed, Corina and I. Ahead of us by a block, he parked his car, stepped out and leaned against the driver side door as he patiently awaited us to walk in his direction. The second I was in front of him, he spoke and asked the usual – name, age, where was I going, etc. He wrote his number down and instructed for me to call him when I got home. Not sure why I did but two days later I found myself at his house in compromising positions.

Our previous phone conversations included talk of me being a virgin – I should have discontinued communication but his in-depth conversation about wanting to de-virgin me left me wanting to allow the 24 year-old man do whatever he saw fit. I skipped school and went to his house. He kissed me in my mouth, while groping my breast and squeezing them through my printed tee, as soon as I walked through the door. Picking me up and carrying me into his room, he told me how he had never tasted fresh, untouched pussy and couldn't wait to slide his tongue deep inside of me. Within three minutes he was in his blue checkered boxers hovering over me as I lay on my back completely naked, breasts pointing directly to the ceiling, feet planted on his mattress with my legs spread apart. I'm not sure what I was getting myself into and at this point it was too late to tell him I wasn't ready for it–he was in control of the situation and I would have to enjoy it or fake it.

Gripping my waist and sliding me down closer to him, he positioned my legs straight in the air, wrapped his right forearm under my waist which caused me to slightly elevate my tail bone off the bed, meeting his lips halfway in mid-air. You would have thought he was face deep in a big slice of watermelon the way he slurped, slobbered, gulped, sucked and spit on my vagina. Unable to contain myself from wiggling around, he removed his arm from under me and proceeded to apply both hands on my inner thigh, pressing down hard while my legs formed an open butterfly position.

Every so often he would come up for his feast and express how good it was, suggesting that this was the pussy he needed in his life forever. He told me fresh pussy like mine was every man's fantasy and he would have to keep it so he could fuck it raw every chance he could. Pitching my clit with his right index and middle fingers each time he popped up to praise his last supper, all I could do was moan, scream and squirm; I don't think he was concerned with my uncomfortable-ness and at this point it was my own fault for allowing myself to be in this position.

Moving his way up to what he called, "the perfect breasts", he used his left hand to assist him as he sucked and juiced up my breasts with his saliva, while fondling around below with my cunt. Starting with his index finger, he applied force and slide it inside of my pussy. Twirling around, touching and leaving his finger print on my walls, his middle finger joined in as the two danced freely inside of me. Occasionally the two formed the peace sign, fingers apart, as a symbolic way of saying goodbye to what I once knew as My Virginity. Stopping all acts he had in play, he quickly removed his boxers and reached over to his brown night stand for a condom. Shuffling around in the top drawer, he paused and stated that he wanted to feel every inch of me on his dick without a glove. He came across as if he was asking but then again he was telling me; staking claim to my untamed pussy was the goal, his mark would be imprinted whether I liked it or not.

Standing up, he slid me to the right corner of the bed and spread my legs open. He told me not to move and that would be gentle upon inserting his penis inside of my vagina. Bending his knees a tad, he grabbed the tip of his dick with his right hand, slapped it on my pussy a few times and proceeded to stick the head in. Quickly pulling it out, he sucked air through his teeth as a sigh of relief and satisfaction before once again introducing his soft tip to the

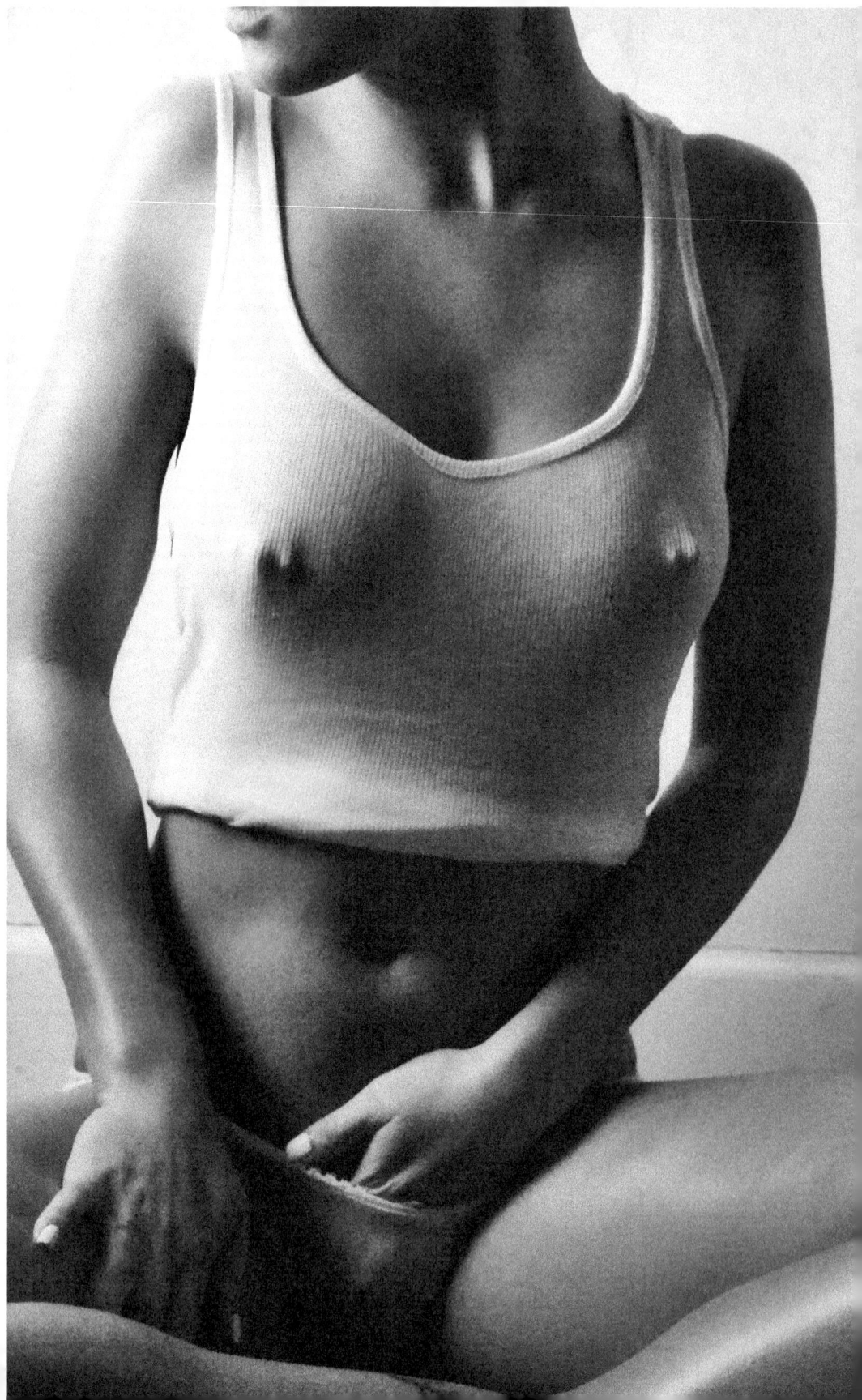

opening of my pink opening while holding the shaft. With just the tip in, he began to stroke the base of his dick while slowly grinding his hips in circular motion. Bringing his left hand to up to caress my left titty, he told me to rock back and forth very slow. Doing as instructed, sliding my ass back and forth on the bed, the second trip forward was met with him completely shoving his dick inside of my cunt. Gasping for air, my heart began to race fast, there was a slight pain felt as he was motionless. No sound or movement came from him as I peeked up and saw his mouth wide open and eyes rolled back to the back of his head.

Finally letting out a noise, he whistled loudly with his lips, looked down at me and proceeded to put his boat in motion. In, out, in and out – I couldn't move, I wanted to scream; I wanted to go home. Oblivious to my discomfort, Leon, continued to stroke my pussy with his dick, even encouraged me to join in by gripping my hips on each side and taking control of my movements. Ten minutes into the act, he said he was about to release, stated my pussy was so good he was setting a new record of ejaculating so fast. I begged for him not to let any get in me, he pulled out his dick, snuggled his dick with his right hand and jacked it off over my navel, while gripping my breasts once again. His conversation about having my pussy forever and molding it to fit his dick, excited him so much, he exploded all over me – navel, stomach and breasts. He asked me to sit up and once doing so, he motioned for his dick to enter my mouth but I shook my head, letting him know I wasn't ready for that.

Making his way to his bathroom to retrieve a wet towel, he wiped my vaginal area and then my upper portion while sincerely telling me I couldn't sleep with anyone else. His wish was granted, as I never did sleep with anyone else. Instead I skipped school on a regular to have sex with him for two more years, causing me to fail many classes while becoming pregnant and losing High School friends in the meantime. Feeling I had a man that would take care of me, I knew I didn't need school. I instead gave birth and became a house girl friend – that was until a new fresh pussy girl came along and he went to satisfying his desire while blaming me for getting him addicted to virgin pussy; choices you make freshmen year can be the downfall to your whole life.

Clit Chronicles: The Officer And The Freak

Fraternizing with an officer of the law was not scheduled on the plans for the day but I'd be lying to myself if I didn't say that I was more than pleased with the actions that corresponded between me and The Man.

Wasn't quite sure why I was being pulled over; registration and inspection tags were up to date. Pulling into a vacant parking lot off the main road, I obeyed the siren alerts. Once parked, I reached over for my insurance forms and license before he approached me. Standing at my window, he informed me that I was being stopped for not coming to a complete halt at the stop sign; I did a "California Stop".

Taking my information and taking a moment to size me up, he stated that he was going to his cruiser to run my information. On his walk back to my window, he walked around my car as if he were inspecting it. Approaching my window, he informed me that my front passenger light was slightly cracked and should get the shield fixed soon. Uncertain what he was speaking of, I requested permission to step out of the car to inspect the minor damage myself; indeed I had damage that I was unaware of. Bending over to get a closer look, it slipped my mind that I was wearing shorts that were short enough to possibly show the frame of my ass if bent over. The officer took notice of the sight before his eyes and let me know he liked what he saw.

Making it clear that he wasn't trying to be rude or abuse his power, he told me he wanted me. Flattered and appreciative of his honesty, giving him what he wanted only seemed like the right thing to do.

Surveying my surroundings, a rush of thrill and adventure took over my body as I faced my car, placed my hands on top of the hood and stuck my ass out in the air. He began to touch my body with his right hand, moving it slowly across my rear and making his way up towards my waist. Joining in with his touch me tease me game, I swayed my hips from side to side, acknowledging I was more than satisfied with what was going on and where it was going. Gripping my waist with both hands, he forced my body to jerk back and forth, causing my ass to hit the front of his pants. With me bent over in front of him, he slid his right hand up to my breasts, fondling them with aggression and passion.

Leaning in towards me while caressing my breasts, the officer kissed the back of my neck. The equipment around his waist got in the way of him really getting into it. He swung me around, pushed me back against the car, causing me to arch my back. Lowering him-self to where his face was met at my stomach. Raising my shirt up, exposing my stomach. Greeting my abs with tender kisses, he found his way to my belly button. Running his tongue around the center of my stomach, he slid his right hand up to grope my right titty, pinching my nipple in the process.

Making his way back down, he grabbed my waist with both hands, massaging my abdomen area with his thumbs. Adjusting his position, he took a step back and ran his right hand across my inner left thigh. Strokes from my thigh to my pussy got me excited and really turned on. I wanted to fuck him right then and there.

Wrestling through my shorts, past my thong and finally to my treasure, he stuck two fingers inside of my pussy. Shoving his fingers deep inside of me, I moved my hips and started fucking his fingers back. Getting deep inside of me, I didn't want this moment to end; my pussy was getting really wet. He took his fingers out of my pussy and brought them up to my mouth. Graciously sucking my sweet juices off of his fingers, I slurped each finger separately.

Taking his fingers from my mouth, he reached down with his right hand for his baton and removed it from its holster. Pushing me back down against my car, he lifted my left leg back on top of the car, pulled my shorts to the side with his left hand and began rubbing his law enforcement club on my pussy. Holding the handle of the baton, he rubbed the side of it up and down my pussy before turning it sideways and pressing the bottom of it on my pussy. Forcefully attempting to stick the baton inside of me, he wanted to use the black club as a dildo and get me off. Not cooperating with him, the baton's corner only found its way inside of me while the rest of it kept sliding out each time he tried to push it in. Possibly my pussy being to wet or the baton just not being made for such sexual acts, he tossed the baton down and began kissing me.

Lifting himself up off of me, he began to remember where he was and his title; he had a shook look on his face. Here he was breaking the law and engaging in public sexual relations with a stranger. He instructed me to fix my clothing as he adjusted himself and picked up his baton.

Walking me back to my door, the kind officer informed me that he would let me go on a warning, this time. He then passed me his business card and told me to stay in touch, making certain to let me know it was more than a sexual connection with us. Not convinced with what he just stated, I was leery on contacting him but I did; it's been 3 years since that day and countless side of the road, handcuff sexual encounters since then.

Clit Chronicles: Loving Every Inch

You surprised me with by coming home early today. I was in the shower doing a little maintenance to my love below; a little trim here, a little trip there, when you pulled back the purple velour shower curtain.

When you stepped into the shower with your clothes fully on, I was taken aback. When you took the green razor from me and kneeled down in front of me, a smile came upon my face. The shower head had the water running on my back so I adjusted it to the left to where it would hit the wall and not be in your way. You lifted my right leg and placed it along the side of the tub so that you could get a good look at "her" and picked up the can of shaving cream, extending your right hand and cuffing my pussy from below, I was too caught up in the moment to realize you eased up on your grip and put the can down. The next thing I felt was you pushing my clit upwards, where you then began to feast on her. Man, she was throbbing something serious!! Trying to let you know how good it felt, my moans were faint when I voiced how good it felt.

You didn't say anything, just continued to lick my clit. Your tongue was moving so fast, it seemed motorized or something. With my right leg still on the tub, you came up, put my right leg down and lifted the left leg onto the soap dish and began to finger my pussy. Even though we were in the shower, you were still able to decipher my natural wetness as my pussy creamed. The anticipation of what was to come got me excited. You looked me in the eyes and as I began to say something, you told me to be quiet. Slightly slipping when you put your whole face against my pussy, you moved your head around and started licking my pussy as if you were an inmate on death

row and it was your last meal. After 10 minutes of being pleased to the point of no return, you stopped and looked up at me with a smile. Your desire to make love to me in the shower quickly shifted once realizing there was no protection anywhere nearby and we both know that sex with no glove was not about to take place.

You instructed me to turn off of the water and to following you – being the submissive person that I am, I obeyed. Searching around for my blue shower towel, you lifted me up and carried me into the room with water dripping off of me onto the floor, leaving a trail. Laying me on the bed, you started taking off of your wet clothes before you began licking the water off of my body; it was such a divine moment. Kissing every inch of my body was so lovely. Turning me over on my back, you caressed it making certain to kiss my shoulders as you whispered that you loved me. Challenging your omission, I advised you to show me just how much you loved me. That's all it took for you to reach into my top night stand drawer and pull a condom out.

Sitting on the edge of the bed in front of me, I was able to see that your dick was so hard; damn it was pretty. The desire to swallow your dick before you put the condom on came over me so I rolled back over to face you, I reached out for your dick as you tried to put the condom on – a quick power struggle with me being the successor, I began to make love to your dick with my mouth. I wanted you deep in my mouth the way you go deep into my wet pussy. I began to suck the tip of your dick the way you love it. With my lips pushed together like a fish I sucked your dick like never before, the taste of your pre cum got me wetter. I allowed my mouth to gather more fluids so it would be wet like my pussy. I began to suck your dick fast, licking the tip of your dick as I reached the top each time and closing my mouth tighter as I reached the bottom. My tongue roaming around in my mouth as I sucked your dick became too much for you, you started popping your toes, reaching for the king size pillow on our bed and making fists with your hands. My knowing I was making you feel good turned me on. With you still sitting on the edge of the bed, I got up and began to straddle you, didn't sit on your dick just yet but you got the drift enough for you to hurry and put the condom on.

With my naked body against yours, holding you real tight, I began to ride up and down on your dick, tightening my pussy walls around you're the tip of your dick as you entered my pussy, each time. I wrapped my legs around your body and began to move faster and faster, you could hear swishing noises from my pussy; she's so wet. You stand up to lay me back on the bed and spread my legs apart before you pushed them up to my shoulders. Looking at your body as you stand over me, I ran my right hand across your beautiful chest. You pulled your body in closer to mine and began to fuck me; yes - FUCK me! I began to scream your name and begged you not to stop. After about 10 minutes of sexing me in this position, you take my left leg and swung it to the right side so that my legs are together and you began to rub my clit and start pounding my pussy; in and out, in and out! With your left hand you smacked my ass so hard, as you know that I love it when you do that. In the same position for awhile, you suddenly asked me to get on my knees. With your dick still inside of me, I twist around and got on my knees, so you could feel all that my pussy had to offer you. I began to move my hips and fuck you back as you open my pussy wider by spreading my lips and fucking me like no tomorrow. I felt you in my stomach; damn your dick is so HUGE. You slowed up as you were about to cum, but you weren't ready to give it up yet. Wanting us to cum the slow grinds and different angles you begin to hit helped the process of me getting closer to my climax. I tightened my pussy around your dick as you went in and out; I'm feeling it now - boy am I EVER feeling it now!! I can't remember the last time I came so hard! You started start fucking me hard and within the next 5 minutes you told me that you were coming. It was as if you read my mind as you pulled out of my pussy, took the condom off and jacked off your dick a little as I turned to face you and suck the tip of your dick hard. You came in my mouth but I didn't stop sucking it as I wanted every drop. When I felt that I had it all, I gave the tip one last good hard suck and swallow, leaving you trembling.

I begin to walk to the bathroom to grab you a towel, I smiled as I thought of the cream feast I just had; ingredients to my lovely treat, water and pineapples.

Clit Chronicles: The Self Pleasure Game

I know I'm wrong for invading her privacy, but she leaves her blinds open all of the time like she wants someone to see her; so just call me nosey. Today was different though, she was walking around in a white bra, with pink ruffles around the trim and a pair of white boy shorts with some sort of rhinestone design on the left side; her body was beautiful. The boy shorts were tight

around the ass and had a unique cut to it so that her ass cheeks hung out the bottom, her ass isn't as big as Buffie the Body's, but it has a cute little heart shape thing going on. I was so memorized I didn't realize she was looking back at me; I'm so embarrassed. I wasn't looking at her with the intent of being a pervert; I'm just nosey as fuck. She began to smile at me, she has a beautiful smile and her eyes have this warm feeling when looking into them. She stood in front of her window facing my direction even more, putting her hand on her hip, looked up an down at her body, then eyes were back on me asking me if I liked what I saw with her eyes. I blinked and took a deep swallow - was she serious? I shook my head and she just smiled even harder.

What am I doing? What is wrong with me? I'm not gay but I can't stop looking at her. All of a sudden I felt my pussy throbbing; what the fuck? Still looking at her, she starts caressing her breast in her bra and gives me a smirk. I looked down towards my pussy and question what it's doing down there. I look back up at her window, I didn't think I looked away that long but I guess I did because she wasn't in front of the window anymore; she could be seen pushing a black leather chair with arm rests, on wheels to the window with a black sharpie in her mouth and a white legal sized note pad on the chair. Once she positioned the chair in front of the window, she took the sharpie out of her mouth and with the note pad, put them on the floor. She sat down in the chair and ran her right hand up and down her right thigh. What did this lady think she was doing? She stood up again, left foot pivoted in front of the right with most of her weight on her right leg; she hit a sexy type pose on me. Switching her weight to her left leg and put her hand on her left hip; striking another pose. She was smiling the whole time, even tossed her hair back some. I couldn't tell if it was a weave or her own hair, but it was long. Her facial features were striking; she had to be a model.

She then turned around, hiked her right knee onto the chair and bent slightly over, with her hands on the arm rests. She looked over her left shoulder back at me and stuck her tongue out, licked her lips and winked at me. She was turning me on. I could feel my pussy getting moist, clit throbbing and nipples getting hard. I just stood there gazing at her beautiful ass in those boy shorts. By this time her shorts made their way into the crack of her ass a little more. She began to move her hips clockwise; she was putting on a show for me. I felt some kind of way when she stopped – disappointed, I suppose. With her back still to me, she reached down and grabbed the sharpie and note pad.

She wrote down something and turned back around, held the paper up; "Sit down & enjoy the SHOW". Okay, this is too much for me, I can't do this. I had an R. Kelly moment; my mind was telling me no – but my body! My body was telling me yes!! Doing as instructed, I looked around for something to sit down on so that I could enjoy the show. The closet thing to me was my boyfriend's piano leather piano stool; fuck it!! I sat down in front of my window, as she did the same. Thank God we were on the 3rd floor and had the only apartments with windows facing out; so many men would be so happy to us.

She sat back in the chair and held another sign up - "Take off your pants". I looked down at my black skin tight jeans with the brown trim and thought about it. I looked back at her and she smiled and nodded at me, as if to say "It's ok". I stood up and began to take my pants off, feeling rather silly I might add. I slid my pants off and revealed my black "Virgo" printed thong - yes I'm a Leo but the Virgo one's were so cute. I sat back down and looked back at her, at this time she placed her right leg on the right arm rest and the left leg on the left arm rest, both feet dangling in the air on each side. She took her right hand, put it in her mouth to moisten her fingers, pulled her boy shorts to the side with her left hand and started rubbing her clit with recently moist fingers. I could see her body squirming in the leather chair, her back arching and ass lifting. She motioned for me to join her but I froze, just sat in awe at what she was doing and how she had my body feeling. She put her index and middle right fingers into her pussy and opened her mouth as if to let a relief of satisfaction out. She then took her left hand and raised it above her head, slightly bent it and ran her hand through her hair, arching her back even more and moving her fingers in and out of her pussy really fast. With her left hand sliding down to her breast, she cuffed the left one and pinched her nipple through her bra, she then started massage her left titty, all while still fingering her pussy. She pulled her feet in together and placed them in the middle of the chair, sort of Indian style, in a diamond shape, not taking her fingers from her pussy or breast though. She reached over to her right breast and pulled it out so that it sat on the outside of the bra; her areola was not too big, not too small, not too dark and not too light - perfect. I began to drool while looking at all she laid out for me to view. The thought came across my mind to join her in this self pleasure game, but I didn't want to miss anything she was doing.

Suddenly I heard keys in door; I jumped up, gave her one last look over and closed the blinds so no one could see that I was being a naughty girl. I quickly put my pants back on and at that very moment, my boyfriend walked in, smiling and happy to see me. I ran to him, kissed him and told him how much I missed him.

We shared more conversation about our day and moved our way into the kitchen so we could decide what to eat for dinner when there was a knock at the door; no one ever knocks at our door. I run to the door and I'm floored to see that it is HER - what was she doing here? She stood at my door way in a black trench coat, black high heels and hair pinned up. I just stood there with my mouth open, shaking my head.

HER: You closed the blinds before I was through. ME: *frantic* My boy friend is home, I'm sorry, I don't know what I was doing it was so out of character for me. You have to go. HER: Boyfriend, aye? Think he would mind us putting on a show for him?

She winked at me when she said that and walked through my front door.

Clit Chronicles: Air Force Lovin'

I don't think I've ever been with someone as sexual as you. Heck, I don't even know if sexual is the word for it, some would say F R E A K Y!! You did things to me last night that I've NEVER in my life done. The evening started off real quiet, you picked me up from my house, and I wore my thigh high khaki colored skirt and white spaghetti strap cleavage shirt. You enjoyed looking at my 36 D breast, so I thought I'd put them on display for you a little. You were still in your uniform, something sexy about an Air Force Pilot in his uniform that turned me on. You mentioned that you just wanted to go home and chill out because your day was long and you knew you had to get up early the next day before your flying out for your next mission; thanks Bush!! We vowed to make every moment be special that night, make it unique.

I loved your house, I still don't know how you managed to get one on Base, everyone knows you have to be damn near married before the let you purchase a house on Base, didn't matter though, I LOVED it and hoped one day I would be able to rest my head here on a regular. You proceeded to walk

downstairs to your bedroom and take your uniform off and slipped some sweats on as I went upstairs to put some music on. I walked into the kitchen to see what we could snack on, nothing but beef jerky in there. You came into the kitchen with me and grabbed a Heineken out of the fridge; booze and women an Air Force man's way to life. I leaned up against the counter and watched you as you looked for some food in the fridge. After searching for a moment, you closed the fridge, turned around towards me and kissed me. Your kisses were rough but passionate; you took your right hand and ran it through my hair, tugging on it hard each time you stroked down. The kisses lead to you sucking on my neck, me moaning, you licking around my neck, me moaning, you licking the top of my breast, me moaning and finally you taking my right breast out of my white laced bra and shirt, putting it into your mouth and sucking it really hard. You looked me deep into my eyes as you continued to suck it, bite it and fondle my left breast with your left hand. Removing your hand and mouth from my breast, you picked me up and laid me on top of the island green marble counter. Sliding your hand up my skirt, hiking it up as your got closer to my pussy, you started rubbing my clit through my white laced thong with your right hand. Taking your left hand, you began to brush my hair back, rubbing my face with your index finger and putting it into my mouth for me to suck.

You slowly started taking off my thong, removed your finger from my mouth and took my skirt completely off, along with my thong. So here I am, lying bottomless on your counter, right titty hanging out of my bra and pussy dripping wet like California's Grizzly Falls and you start drinking your Heineken, and I couldn't help but laugh. A smirk came over your face, looked as if you had an idea or something. Next thing I know you take Heineken, tilt towards me and poured its contents over my pussy, and worked its way down to my ass crack. Putting the beer bottle down, you spread my legs further apart and started licking the beer from my pussy, getting real sloppy with it, like your tongue had a mind of it's on. It felt so good, I started arching my back some so you could get to the pussy real good, then you took your right hand and started massaging my titty that was hanging out. You went to work on my pussy for a good 15 minutes when another idea came to your head. You picked up the beer bottle, took your left hand, parted my pussy lips and inserted the Heineken bottle into my wet pussy.

Ok, this is a first, a green beer bottle in my pussy, I didn't stop you though I just laid back, opened my legs more and allowed you to play with me the way you wanted to. Twisting the beer bottle to the left and right each time you stroked it in and out felt really good. I guess you wanted to make it a feeling I'd never forget once you started rubbing my clit with your index and middle fingers really fast. This sensation was too much for me and I felt myself trembling, I was about to cum. I told you I couldn't take it anymore, but you knew it was all talk; you had to know because you didn't stop. After 10 more minutes of fucking me with the Green Heineken bottle I exploded harder than I've ever cum before, my cum was squirting in the bottle like milk from a cow in a bucket.

I couldn't move, just laid there breathing really hard and wondering what in the hell just happened. I looked up at you and that look came over your face again; idea!! You took the beer bottle out of my pussy and raised it to your mouth, oh wow!! With too huge gulps my sweet cum was swallowed and a smile of satisfaction came across your face. Putting the beer bottle down you carried me downstairs and made love to me with your dick 5 times that night, each time me coming harder and harder. By the end of the night, my pussy was so swollen, looked as if she had gotten into a fist fight with Mike Tyson or something, it was all worth it though. I knew in my heart that when you took off the next day to go to Germany, I'd be on your mind, in your heart and in your system - literally, until you came back home.

Clit Chronicles: High School Love

Gosh, I can't believe I'm dating the most popular guy in High School. Here I am 14 and I got me a 16 year old, a man all the chicks in school want. I think he's more experienced then I am though, like sexually, I'm not sure though. What if he asks me to sex him? I've never done that. Will I bleed when I do have sex? Will I really feel my cherry pop? Hell, what does my Cherry look like? Is there a way to see it before its popped? Why am I so concerned about that? He hasn't even asked me about sexing him or anything.

We normally hang out with all of our friends and do stupid stuff like cut school and ride the train all throughout the City. I often go to his Basketball games and before each game I allow him to rub my breast; they aren't that big, but he said it's for good luck - he always has a good game!! Game days are normally the days a group of us cut class and have fun, kind of the boy's way of clearing their mind before the game. Seeing as how they were in the Championships, I'd say the rides and stuff worked, hell something did. So this game day was just like any other, we did the usual. This particular day however, I wanted to wear something cute, I secretly wanted him to have better access to my breast. I didn't have many cute clothes, but my best friend did so when I went to her house before school I got some clothes from her dryer. I found this red body suit and a dark blue denim skirt with a split up front, sort of had a ash wash fade to it. I knew my Boy Friend would love this outfit; it wasn't every day I got cute for him.

We sat in the 1st car on the train; no one was really around us but the conductor. We were loud, so we didn't want to be around too many people. One of our friends asked if we wanted to play truth or dare, the game started of innocently until people started daring us to do sex things. Someone dared my best friend to rub a friends dick head through his pants, someone dared our guy friend to put a finger in my best friends pussy, someone dared me to sit on my boy friend's lap and grind on his penis and someone dared others to do other titty feeling, dick rubbing, pussy rubbing things. Then out of the blue, my best friend dared my boy friend to lick my pussy, I was shocked and was thinking of how nasty that is.

My boy friend looked around, I guess for a place to lay me down, because next thing I know he grabs my hand and takes me to an area where 2 long seats are facing one another, with floor space between them. He asked that everyone gather around and cover us up as he laid me on the floor, at that moment I remembered I was wearing pink and purple flowered panties - who wore shit like that in High School!??! Everyone comes around us and my boy friend spreads my legs apart, pulls my panties down to my ankles. The next thing I felt was his thumb pushing up against my clit and his tongue licking my clit. I don't know how, but it felt like he was wrapping his tongue around it. I heard "ohhh's" and "awww's" from our friends and I couldn't believe this was happening. Next he let his tongue hang out completely and licked my labia; he kept kicking it over and over again, each time getting sloppier and sloppier with it. I felt his saliva fall down the crack of my ass and for a moment I forgot I was surrounded by my peers on the train getting my pussy licked. I was so taken a back with the techniques he displayed; he lifted my ass up in

the air from the bottom, raising it to his eye level and began to lick my pussy, licking the insides of my walls - one at a time.

I couldn't take it anymore, I started feeling all hot all over my body, had to make him stop. I quickly sat up and made him stop. Everyone around us took a step back and stood there with gasp looks on their faces. Then people started cheering and rooting my boy friend on to do it again, gosh, my friends were perverts. Everyone took a seat on the two chairs we had just laid between and started the game up again. My pussy was still moist from the treatment it just received, I found myself moving around in my seat and couldn't control it. My boy friend noticed my movement and kneeled down in front of me, asked me to spread my legs apart and relax my jaw - a relaxed jaw means an open vagina. I did as I was told; he took my right hand and placed it in my panties, having my fingers soak up the wetness that was being released from my pussy. He took control of my hand and made circles around my clit with my full hand. I don't think this is something we should be doing in front of our friends, but it felt too good to stop him. I closed my eyes, I don't know for how long, just knew that when I opened them my boy friend was jacking his dick off in front of me and was saying he was about to cum - uhh ok!! With his hand still on top of my hand in my wet pussy he continued to stroke his dick with his left hand, slightly curling his index finger over the tip each time he went up and the suddenly he came all over his stomach. It caught me off guard, I stopped what I was doing and out of the blue someone dared my best friend to lick the cum off of his stomach - okay, these fuckers are getting out of control now. I'll be damned if my best friend puts her lips anywhere close to my boy friend. The next thing we hear is yelling..

GROWN UP: What are you kids doing? BOY FRIEND: Oh shit, let's go ya'll. We all jumped up and ran to the nearest door, luckily the train was at a stop and we were able to get off. My panties were still moist, I don't know what my boy friend did about the cum on his stomach, we just booked out of there. Needless to say, things with he and I changed a whole lot, I felt rushed into what we had started and didn't want to go further, so we broke up. I think I'll wait until I'm married to do anything like that again - I hope.

Clit Chronicles: Why Settle For One?

I don't know what came over me tonight, I was like taken over by someone else - had to be. I'm in my 1998 Gray Grand Prix with a guy I've been seeing for a while, well not really seeing, it's been more of a "he eats me out really good type thing". He wasn't exactly a looker, actually he was ugly and the only reason I gave him the time a day was because he licked pussy so well and I was drunk the first night he did it and been sprung every since. Hell, it's not like I'm in a relationship or even seeing someone else, a girl has needs and if I don't have to fuck to get one off, damn skippy I'm going to get my pussy licked.

So we're in my car, in the front seat in front of his house laughing at some movie we had just seen, yes I actually hung out with the fat fuck. I only did it because I was in need of some pussy licking attention. He had 2 of his boys in the house who were extra loud and annoying, so we sat in the car, it was a good enough place for him to do his thing. He reached over from the passenger seat and started rubbing my thigh; I was wearing a black mini skirt and a white baby phat mid drift tee. I was turned sideways facing the steering wheel, but felt it was time for me to face him in some manner. I positioned my body, putting more weight on the right side and turned towards him, he put his hands deeper into my skirt and found the gold he was searching for. I wasn't wearing any panties so it was easy for him to get down to it. He stuck his thumb in my pussy, turned it sideways and began moving it in and out. I wanted him to get in deeper, so I lifted my right leg up and rested it on the center arm console and my left leg rose on top of the dashboard. With him still using his right thumb and fucking me with it, he takes his left hand and starts rubbing my clit. I start moving my hips, letting him know that I enjoyed what he was doing, and pushing my body in towards him each time he stuck his thumb inside my pussy. he removed his thumb from my pussy, still rubbing my clit, brought his face down closer to my pussy and began to suck it - almost felt like he bit it. I don't know how he managed to get my whole pussy in his mouth, but his mouth covered my whole fucking pussy, pussy lips and all. He managed to put his tongue inside my pussy, licking the inside walls. He took slow, deep strokes with his tongue, pushing it deep inside my pussy every now and then. The sensation of him rubbing my clit and licking my pussy the way he did was too much for me, I came all in his mouth. He removed his hand, but continue to suck my pussy, he was sucking it as if he was dry to suck it dry getting every drop if cum out, reminded me of sucking a green olive and sucking the red eye out of it.

He finally came up for air and had a look of fullness over his face. That shit felt so good I wanted more, I wasn't satisfied yet, I need to feel a his huge black dick inside of me, but then again there was NO way I was going to let his double belly ass stick his dick in me. A thought came into my head; his boys were fine, why not fucking them.

ME: Let's do something different tonight. How about we go inside and have fun with yo boys. I didn't have to repeat myself, he got up so quickly, got out of the car and walked around to my side and opened my door. As we walked into the house i began to get nervous, I hope these dudes had condoms or this was NOT going down. He took me into the downstairs bedroom, his house was a huge 4 bedroom house and his boys were in the living room next to the room he took me too. I lay across the bed spread, opened my legs and began to rub my pussy, it turned him on. He left out the room as I laid there and rubbing my pussy, came back 2 minutes later with his boys. They looked at me and I could tell they were down, hell, I'm a pretty fly bitch if I don't say so myself. They looked at him and questioned if he was for real, he nodded towards me and I gave them a smile, while still rubbing my pussy but cuffing my breast now too. One of his boys walks over to me and helps me with my pussy, sticking two fingers inside of me as I'm rubbing my clit, the other walks over and lifts up my shirt, pulls my right titty out of my bra and begins to suck on it. My friend looks at the satisfaction on my face, walks into a closet, comes back out with a camera in his hand - okay, this is REALLY a first. He begins to snap pictures of me being pleased by his two friends. Friend #2 starts biting hard on my nipples as #1 puts four fingers in my pussy, beating my pussy walls up. My friend comes over, rolls me on my left side while the other two boys do their thing, licks his index finger and sticks in it my ass hole. So here I am laying on my left side, got a dude sucking my right titty and fondling the left, another dude finger fucking my pussy and one finger fucking my ass, wow, no wonder I came within two minutes of the finger in my ass.

Friend #1 tells me he wants to fuck me, I'm down for that but tell him he's going to have to strap up first. He gets up off the bed, and reaches into his back pocket, pulls his wallet out and retrieves a condom. Friend #2 has taken over the fingering of the pussy job and Friend 31 puts the condom on and my friend is still working on my ass - two fingers inside now, twisting and turning as he goes in and out. Friend #1 walks back over to the bed with nothing but a white tee and white socks on, takes my hand and messes up the groove the other two men had going on. He stands me up and walks me to the foot of the bed, he sits on the bed and sits me on top of him. He cuffs my titties and begins fucking me, man that shit felt good. Friend 32 walks over, looks at me, points to his dick and then at me - as if to ask if I'd suck him up, fuck it, why not. He unbuckles his pants and pull his underwear and pants down to his ankles, dick was hard as a rock. I wanted to examine it, but it was too dark and the fuck action I had going on wouldn't allow me to concentrate on that, I just grab the dick and began sucking. I start out with an open mouth suck, letting my mouth get moist a little before I start sucking it hard and slow. Keeping up with the dick inside of me, I tighten my pussy walls on the dick as he goes in and out. Out of no where I feel hands around my waist and I'm being pulled back a little, Friend #1 opens his legs a little more and allows me to fall freely some, but not losing his rhythm. The hands I felt were of my friend and he some how managed to get up under me in a crab position and was fucking me in the ass. He had his hands on the floor, which was holding him up and began to give me hard pelvic thrusts. This shit was turning me on for real now, I began to suck and jack of the dick I had in my mouth so hard, he came all in my mouth. I allowed him nut to run out of my mouth and down my breast when all of a sudden Friend #1 lifted me and laid back on his back, putting my knees on the mattress which made my ass in the air and free to be fucked doggy style by my friend. I don't know how they managed this position, they were pretty much holding me up, I had NO more control of my body.

I don't know what happened to Friend #2, I just remember my friend cumming and nutting all over my ass,me cumming one last HARD time and Friend #1 nutting inside the condom and telling me how good my pussy was and that I was a trooper to take all 10 inches of him. I must have passed out but woke up a few hours later in the room alone, smelling fresh with a white tee on. I looked around and gathered my things and snuck out of the house. The next day I was told that my friend had bathed me, put one of his tees on me and laid me in the bed. He said he was shocked to find me gone when he woke up, I expressed to him that I was embarrassed and he told me I need not be, no one thought any less of me. I couldn't really take his word on that so after that conversation we never spoke again. Yeah, I miss the good pussy licking loving he used to give me, but hey, I'm sure I'll experience it again.

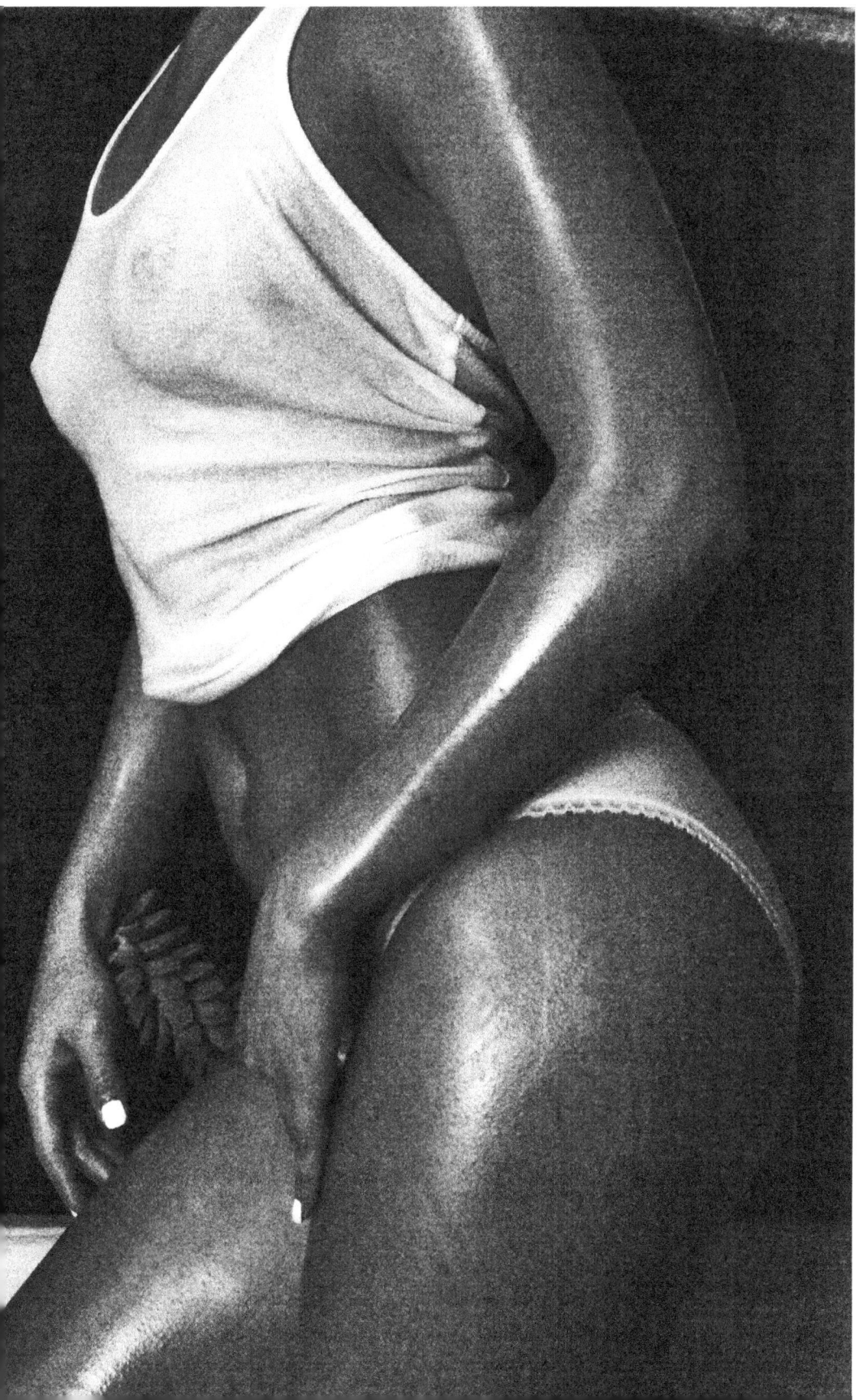

Clit Chronicles: Piano Love

I don't know what made me want to hear Brian Mc Knight, I guess the fact that I wasn't feeling well and a little depressed could have been my reason. I didn't even know what time it was, felt like 4am though. You were already up, you said you couldn't sleep so you decided to play on the computer a little. I was missing you in the room, we always lay in the bed touching one another in some way, so I decided to come out front and lay on the couch to be closer to you. You stopped what you were doing as I walked past you and looked at me walking around the house with a white tee shirt and my white fleece blanket. You asked me why I was up, of course I said because you were. You swung around in your black leather computer chair and faced me as I stood in front of you, I reached out to your face with my right hand and ran it across your cheek, it was then I asked you to play me some Brian Mc Knight.

You were thrown off by my request, considering it was so late, yet so early, but you complied. You rose from your chair, wearing your gray sweats with no shirt, and walked to your piano. I remember our first date, you called yourself impressing me by playing the piano for me, Brian was one of the songs you played then and never played since. Sitting down in your black leather stool now, you begin to play "Back at One", man I wish you could sing to me. So many memories of our first date came back to me, I wanted to cry. After that song, you started playing Alicia keys, followed by some KC & Jo Jo, a few other things; even some Classical, and finally ended with another Brian Mc Knight song. When you played KC & Jo Jo, "All My Life" I felt myself crying, thinking of the words to the song was exactly how I felt about you; I waited for someone like you all my life. I have you in my life and I feel like I'm about to lose you, it killed me.

Around the time you started playing the Michael Jordan commercial theme song I started feeling horny, go figure. I wasn't wearing any panties under my tee shirt because I remove them and my panties while sleeping at night. Laying on my stomach, I turned side ways, laying on my left side, bent my right knee up some, licked my right index and middle finger and began to rub my clit. The sounds coming less than 5 feet away from me were turning me on, I started moving my body in sync with the music. Spreading my pussy lips apart with my index and right ring finger, I began to finger myself with my middle finger and rub my clit with my thumb. I pictured your hands rubbing

me up and down my body, caressing each inch. I wished you would touch me with such passion as your fingers stroked the keys on your key board, such grace, love , concentration and dedication. The Classical music did me in, picturing your fingers moving fast across the key board, being detailed and precise about each stroke, I wanted that same attention. I began to moan a little, but I don't think you heard me, still moving my hips to the music I started rubbing my clit really fast with my index and middle fingers. Arching my back and grinding in the air, I can feel it, I'm about to cum. I started picturing your fingers rubbing my clit as you played the last Brian Mc Knight song; gosh I want you so badly. And finally I came, it felt so good!! After completing my mission, I stood up, walked over to you and started caressing your shoulders and kissed you on the back of your head. You turned around, raised up and told me it was time to go back to bed, you only had an hour and a half left to get rest before work. We walked hand and hand down the hallway to our bedroom and made our way into our king sized bed. I don't know what made you walk over to my side of the bed, we both know you always lay closest to the door, I didn't complain though. You laid in the bed and held me, we talked a little and I told you how you hadn't played Brian for me since our first date. I thanked you for playing it for me, I then told you I loved you, you said the same and we fell asleep in one another's arms as the sun begin to rise. You made love to me with your music today and you have no idea how much I enjoyed it.

Clit Chronicles: I'll Always Have Memories

I can't believe you're lying next to me, after the things we have been through I never saw this coming. The fact that I haven't been feeling good and you stayed with me was comforting. Having you around hasn't really been a huge deal to me, until tonight. Lying in my bed, tossing and turning, I have thoughts of you holding me. I remember the night you kissed every inch of my body after a long day; I wish you would do that again. Starting with my toes, you began sucking on my big toe, I recall how it tickled. I pulled my foot back but you didn't stop hell I don't think I really wanted you to. You kissed the tip of every toe on my right foot, and then worked your way to my left foot. From there, sweet kisses on my left ankle, shin, knee, and thigh were given by you. You did the exact same on my right side. Every time you got to my pussy you just teased me with THOUGHT of kissing it. Up my belly to my right breast and down my right shoulder, arm and down to my finger tips – same attention to the left side. You asked me to turn over so you could give my back side the same attention and love. When you made it to the middle of my back I found myself gripping the thick blue comforter that was spread on our bed, the feeling was intense. The kisses on the back of my neck were arousing and had me wanting to make love to you. I turned over to face you and started kissing you; the only time we really kiss is when we're getting it on. You started cupping my right titty with your right hand, massaging it, caressing it. I started working my hands down to your lower half searching for the hidden treasure. You caught on to what I wanted and asked me if I wanted it. I replied, "Fuck yeah". You took your boxers off as I laid there with my legs open rubbing my clit impatiently waiting for your magic stick. I don't think we've ever made love without a condom, but I guess today was a special night. Maybe it was the fact that you knew I was dripping wet and couldn't wait for you to walk to the closet, get your wallet and find a condom because you just gave me all of your love. You've always been a perfect fit inside my pussy, she just grips it with no problem. Slowly you move in and out of me allowing my juices to slip out to the outside world onto our bed, didn't matter to me though, this was worth me cleaning tomorrow. You started getting more into it, running your fingers through my hair, smiling the whole time. Everything about you is so perfect and beautiful.

You started repositioning yourself so you could get deeper in me, I thought you were trying to do your trademark move that I love so much but you just swung my right leg on top of my left and started hitting it sorta side ways. After about ten minutes of me telling you how much I loved your dick you switched on me again. You never took your dick out of me when you spun around and got in a 69 position, this is new!! With me laying flat in my back and you laying flat on your stomach on top of me, legs straight out to the top of my head, you pushed yourself into me. I don't think I've ever felt you this deep inside of me. I could tell by the way you were moving that this was a new position for you, not to mention the moaning you were doing; you're normally quiet until you explode. So here we are in this new position and I feel myself cumming, I tell you and you start pushing in me faster, I lift me legs up and spread them apart some so that your chest is on the bed but legs still close to my ears. You start giving it to me harder telling me you want me to cum all over the dick I love so much. I can't recall ever cumming like that; it was different in a wonderful way. You didn't stop giving me the sausage until you felt yourself cumming, at this point you scooted back so that your dick was hovering over my face and guided your dick into my mouth. Licking my juices off your dick always turned you on. You came instantly and I sucked as hard as I could, you like for me to keep sucking until I swallow your cum and that's what I did. We both got what we wanted this night.   That night was a special night and will always be remembered, its no wonder if crosses my mind right now. We may never have another night like that but you should know it will never be forgotten. I lay with you at this very moment wanting to hold your hand or something. I guess you being the most important person in my life this way are better than not having you in my life at all. I'm not hopeful for anything in the future other than being a friend, but the thoughts of our great sex life will always be in my heart. Those are memories that cannot be touched.

Clit Chronicles: Make Me Squirt

My boy, Jay, ran an afterhours spot in Detroit. A gang of dudes would come through one of his houses on the East side and watch us girls dance all night for them. I was most of the guy's favorite, because I demanded respect and wouldn't get completely naked for them, they all called me, "CALI" because that's where I'm from. I have a small frame; 5'5, 135, 36C breast, perfect 6 pack stomach and a cute little heart shaped booty. I had this signature move I did where I would sit on a guys lap, wrap my legs around the bottom of the chair (it had to be a folding chair), fall back so my pussy was in the air, let my arms go free over my head and roll my hips on the guy. The house had 3 different rooms; living room was the main room where all the dancing went on, the first bedroom was where a few sexual acts went down and the second bedroom was where the FUCKING went on. You would NEVER catch me in the other two rooms, didn't have to, I'm CALI!

Candi and I were in the second room changing clothes, wasn't much in the room but a bed and a dresser. She had a nice thick ass on her, was light skinned with long brown hair, had to be a B cup, but again her ass was FAT! She put on a fishnet lace crotch-less body suit and I put on a pair of blue thongs, a blue and white halter top with a white, tight fitting skirt over my thong. Candi and I were talking about the crowd and wanted to put on a good show tonight. She asked me how free I was and if I was down to try anything? I was a lil thrown off and quickly let her know I wasn't down for having sex with any of those men. She them asked if I would have sex with her as she walked towards me. My eyes grew and my clit started throbbing, what was going on? She reached out with her right hand and began rubbing my right breast, cupping it, pulling it from the side of my top and massaging my nipple. She took her left hand and began rubbing my pussy. I just stood there in awe, couldn't believe what was going on. She stood face to face with me and stuck her tongue out and started moving it up and down on my lips. The throbbing sensation coming from my pussy had me so excited I just wanted to lay down and let her have her way with me. Still standing, she continued to rub my pussy, she was rough with it but it turned me on. With her left hand cuffed on my pussy she took her middle finger to pull my thong to the side and worked her index finger inside my pussy. Her right hand was working its way back and forth between my breast, massaging and cuffing. She then pushed me down onto the bed really hard with her right hand and spread my legs apart. Looking up to the ceiling I couldn't believe the events that were happening.

Candi pulled me to the edge of the bed and stood between my legs over me. She kneeled down in front of me, pulled my thong to the side with her left hand and began licking my pussy. I think everyone female goes through their curious stage, ya know, being with another female. Most females won't admit to it but we all are curious. She went to work on my pussy and I almost felt like I had been missing out on something all my life. She turned her left hand upside down and pressed it up against my pussy, having the lips and clit between her index and middle finger, began sticking her tongue deep into my pussy and licking the walls. I found myself grinding my pussy into her face as if I were riding it. She took her face out of my pussy and began sticking her left index and middle finger in my pussy, twisting it turning it as she worked it in and out. I started moaning really loud, almost screaming. Jay came in the room to check on us and was shocked to see what was going on, I heard him say, "Damn! Get that shit!" Candi didn't stop what she was doing, just keep fucking my pussy with her fingers and sucking my clit so hard. I felt myself cumming, I couldn't hold it anymore. I told her I was about to cum, well yelled to her I was cumming. I noticed Jay standing in the doorway rubbing his dick as I began to cum. I've never cum so hard in my life, I began squirting all over the bed, that has never happened to me. Felt like I was a cow being milked the way my cum came shooting out. All I could do was scream until every last drop was out, I noticed Candi licking up and trying to catch my cum. There was no way I was going to be able to dance after experiencing something like that, I just wanted to lay there all night and sleep. I told Jay I needed a lil more time and he understood, he and Candi left me in the room and I fell asleep. About an hour later, Candi came back in to check on me and it was on again. Man, I think I fell in love with her that night. Actually, I know I did, we've been hot and heavy for 4 years now and I still squirt every night.

Clit Chronicles: Just say NO to Driving and Cumming

I finally met a man who knows how to stimulate me in other ways besides using his dick. For some reason men think that having a big dick and beating it up against my walls really hard is what makes a woman come - not the case! Ruben did some things to me that made me want to slap my Momma!! He stimulated parts of my body that I didn't know existed, muscles being used that hadn't been in years.

Ruben and I were traveling back from Borders Book Store (I just had to pick up Eric Jerome Dickey's latest book, Chasing Destiny) when he reached over to the passenger seat with his right hand and started rubbing my left thigh. I guess he felt he had easy access since I was wearing a knee length blue jean skirt, but Kelly doesn't play that. I playfully pushed his hand away with my left hand and told him to stop. I knew what he was trying to do, he wanted to get me all hot and bothered, take me home and fuck the living shit out of me, but I wasn't having that. He reached over one last time, this time getting a little further than the last. He started sliding his hand up and down, caressing my thigh and rubbing my knee; okay, I'm turned on now. Ruben stopped what he was doing and began pulling the car over into a Wendy's parking lot. After stopping the car, he stepped out and walked to my side of the car. Opening my door he told me to get out and told me to drive. I thought he was tripping at first because he has never asked me to drive his car, it's a 01 MERCEDES BENZ s430 and you know how men are with their cars. I complied and did as he requested, after adjusting my seat and fixing the mirror's I pulled out of the parking lot and started back on the road.

I hadn't been driving for more than 2 minutes when I noticed him fidgeting around his seat, but I just figured he was adjusting it right. Reaching over to my side with his left arm on the neck rest and right hand on my thigh, he worked his way into my skirt and pulled my thong to the side. I guess he knew what I was thinking, wondering what had come over him to 1st allow me to drive his Benz and now him fondling me as I'm driving it, because he whispered for me to relax. Trying to keep my eye on the road and remain calm I blocked out what he was doing and then suddenly I hear a buzzing sound coming from behind my seat. Bringing his left arm around to the side of me, while his right hand was parting my pussy lips under my skirt, I noticed he was holding some sort of device; a vibrator. Not just any kind of vibrator though, a silver mini bullet! Pulling his hand from between my legs, he switched the vibrator to his right hand and had it take the place his hand. The vibration inside my pussy was a great sensation; tingly yet comforting. Ruben adjusted the controls to make the speed increase which made me shift and adjust myself in the seat some; rolling tail bone from left to right and right to left. I felt my juices trickling down my ass as my head fell back onto my neck rest and rolling off; I came so hard.

Driving and enjoying this feeling was going to get us killed so I looked around for some place for me to pull over; saw an Elementary school and felt it would do. Parking the car I immediately laid my seat back, lifted my left leg on the dash board, raised my skirt up and pulled my thong to the side even more. Ruben laughed at me because I had did everything so fast; moved like a crack head who had just lucked up and found a piece of crack on the ground, I wanted more!! He grabbed me up under my butt and turned me towards him, spreading my legs apart so that one was behind the passengers head rest and the other was propped on the dashboard and head pushed up against the door handle. Ripping my thong completely off, Ruben pulled a 7 inch vibrator with a curve at the end of it from under his seat. Pushing the sensual teaser inside my pussy, I closed my eyes, raised my hips up and started thrusting my body in his direction. My ass kept hitting the center console but I didn't care, I just kept thrusting. Ruben took his left hand and ran his index finger under the vibrator collecting some of my juices onto it. With cream he got from me, he began rubbing my exposed clit with his left index and middle finger. With the vibrator going in and out of me and his fingers running circles over my clit I came again and again.

Just as I was getting back focused from my 3rd nut there was a tap on the passenger window; it was a Police Officer. Oh snap! One would think that

I would have been embarrassed but I was HIGH; high like Whitney Houston. Bringing my legs back together and adjusting myself in my seat, Ruben rolled his window down and gave the Officer a smirk. He asked what we were doing and I gave him a dumb look. He walked up to the window and saw my pussy spread all out in the open and he's asking what we were doing, ha! Ruben apologized to him, not even answering the question and told him it wouldn't happen again. The Officer gave us a verbal warning and told us to drive safe. As we pulled out of the parking lot we both burst into laughter, now this was one to wait home about. Speaking of home, this man has NO idea of the things I'm going to do to him once I get him there; it's ON!!

Clit Chronicles: MySpace is the Devil!

I'm never one to want to meet a man from a web site or dating site and want to sleep with him the first day of meeting him, but lately I've come across this one guy who I just HAVE to have!! Sure I've gone out with men from different sites and hung with them, but never have I given it up to them the first night. I blame this shit on TOM and MySpace for this feeling I have now!!

Daryl is so GORGEOUS, not to mention really nice and friendly. I've never talked to a Haitian guy before, never had sex with one and I must say I'm rather curious!! I enjoy receiving messages from him and he's always leaving me the cutest comments on my page; he just brightens up my day. For the past two weeks we have become a little closer, holding phone conversations and even becoming number one on his friends list; yes, I'm moving on up! Our conversations are starting to get more personal and deep now, very sexual even. After talking to him today chills came across my body, my heart started beating fast and my pussy began throbbing. He told me he wanted to taste me and jokingly said "I bet you taste like Chicken." I want this man so bad I'm DYING inside! Fuckin MySpace - I hate you!!

Daryl ran across my mind this morning after my shower, just thinking of him and the things he said he wants to do to me drive me nuts!! With nothing but a towel around me, I went to my computer, clicked onto his MySpace page and viewed his pictures. His smile is so exquisite and presentable, I decided to print his picture out. With his printed picture I laid across my couch and began to explore my body and day dream about the man who's picture was

laying to my right shoulder. With my left hand I started spreading my pussy lips apart, envisioning him with his head between my legs spreading my lips with his left hand. Licking the tip of my right index and middle fingers I brought it down and began rubbing my clit, envisioning it was his tongue and he was flickering my clit with the tip of his pointy tongue. I wish I could push his face deep into my pussy and have his thick, soft lips cover my pussy as he slides his tongue inside touching, moving it from left to right hitting the side walls of my vagina. Me contracting my muscles and moistening his tongue with my Chicken flavored pussy. Him making noises as he slurps my juices up and rolling his tongue inside my pussy as if he were eating an ice cream cone. Oh how I would just love for him to take his arms and wrap them under and around my upper thighs, lifting me off the couch some but closer to him with a tight grip so I can squirm away. I want to roll my hips, grip the back of his ears and make love to his tongue. Just the thought of him eating me out makes me smile and closer to orgasm. Imagining him licking my clit like a kitten washing themselves and sliding his right index and middle finger inside of me, jerking me off really fast and hard, making me moan and wiggle; oh I want him so bad. Why TOM Whyyyyyyyyyy?!! I just want him to use his fingers and fuck me until I cum. Just twist his fingers inside me, rubbing his thumb up against my clit each time he strokes inside me.

I can't believe I'm laying on my couch day dreaming sexually of a man I've never met about to cum. I glance over my right shoulder at his picture and get closer to my point. Reaching over to grab his picture with my left hand, hold it in front of me and moan his name. I close my eyes and picture him smiling at me, whispering for me to cum for him and asking if my pussy was his. "Yes, Yes, it's all yours!!" Grinding my hips into the air, I take his picture and place it between my legs, pushing the paper close to my pussy as I cum. Yelling as loud as I could, releasing everything inside of me, was just a relief. I want that man so bad I don't want him. There's NO way I can meet him, I'll be a slut! I'm not a slut, man!! Fuckin TOM!! I hate you!!

Clit Chronicles: Did It For The Stories

I went to go visit my boy friend, Craig, at University of California Berkeley where he lived on campus with his room, Chris. Their apartment, if you want to call it that was REALLY small and crammed, more like a one bed room with a bed in the living room, which was Craig's domain. It had been 3 weeks since I saw him and I couldn't wait to feel his luscious lips pressed up against mine. That wasn't the only thing I wanted while up there, but it was the most important.

Seeing Craig as I stood at the bottom of his stairwell filled my heart with so much joy; I rushed to him and kissed him passionately. In between our tongues connecting he mumbled that my kisses felt good. I didn't take my eyes off of him, just reached out with my right hand and ran it across the top of his head. It all felt so unreal and I wanted to touch him to make sure I wasn't dreaming. He lifted me up and twirled me around in the air, never breaking the kissing action we had going on; felt good to see him. As we made our way upstairs to his spot, he reached out with his right hand for my left hand and gave me the grand tour of their castle. I noticed the bedroom door was closed and inquire as to why, he told me that Chris was in there studying. I didn't know Chris too well, but we had talked a few times on the telephone. As we made our way back into the front room, I sat down on the right side of his red oak sleigh bed as he walked around and sat on the left. He spread himself across the bed lying with his head at the foot of the bed with his arms spread apart. He reached his arms out to me, as to ask me to come to him and lay with him and I complied. Lying on my left side on his left arm felt really good but got even better as he reached over with his right hand and gripped my hair into his fist as if it were a pony tail and began kissing me on the back of my neck. He knew that was my spot and I had no idea what he was trying to get started. I giggled as I told him to stop and pointed to the closed bedroom door, as to remind him that Chris was home. I guess he thought about it and didn't want to make me uncomfortable so he stopped. We just laid there for another hour in one another's arms until he dozed off. It had been a while since I had a chance to watch him sleep so peacefully so I lifted myself up, turned around slightly and glanced at him; sleeping like a baby. A smile of happiness ran across my face as I thought about all the happy times we've shared together.   I began looking around the apartment. Taking another look at the closed bedroom door I figured there was really no way Chris would come out if I behaved badly. For some reason I didn't care anymore that there was someone in the house, I guess it would just be a story the boys could share amongst themselves if it came down to it; I was feeling horny and wanted my man. Reaching my left arm across his body and applying all of my weight onto it, I carefully began to unbutton & unzip his jeans, slowly. I didn't want to awaken him until the RIGHT moment. With the top of his pants open, I slide my left hand into the slit of his boxers and pulled his dick out, I did it fast because I knew he would awaken and by the time he knew what was going on it would be in my mouth. Sure enough as soon as my warm mouth was about to hover his dick he flinched some, that didn't stop me though, I was going to complete my mission. Sticking my tongue out and sliding his dick into my mouth and huge grin came upon his face as I looked at him with my eyes rolled to the top of my head. He was about to say something but I quickly took my left hand and covered his mouth with my index finger. Slightly losing my balance, I took the time to reposition myself; bringing my knees together and sitting on them in between his legs. With his arms still spread out and me in between his legs, he slightly lifted his head up and mouthed, "What are you doing?". I continued what I was doing and paid him no attention. Closing my eyes and sliding his dick further into my mouth, I placed the tip of my tongue on the tip of his penis, expanding his hole. Stroking his dick right my right hand, I continue to stimulate his opening with my tongue, sliding it in a little further. Removing my tongue from this spot and now focusing on his dick as a whole, I watered my mouth with saliva and began devolve his dick into it. Sucking the tip of his dick and expanding my mouth form as I reached the bottom of his dick was a technique I knew he loved. Him bringing his legs up some let me know I was doing a good job. Continuing my mission I decided to focus on just the tip pf his dick, I knew that was the key to me getting the treasure I was looking for; his cum flowing on the inner walls of my mouth. Twisting my head from side to side as I sucked the tip of his dick, squeezing my cheeks together, making a "pop" sound each time I released the grip around his dick when I reached the top. I hadn't gotten the full effect of his taste before he reached up, pulled me towards him and began kissing me. Stroking his dick with my right hand as we're kissing, he took his left hand and stopped me. Never taking away my kisses, he started fumbling around with my jeans to unfasten them. Pulling away from his mouth I sat up and quickly undid my pants myself. As I was doing that, Craig reached under his mattress and retrieved a mint green color wrapped lifestyle condom; I was too caught up in the moment to ask him where in the fuck was the box for the condoms.   He slid the condom on as I removed my pants and panties. Reaching out for me to climb on top of him I spread my legs apart, licking my right hand, sliding it across my pussy and hopped aboard. It had been a while so I pushed him inside of me gently; letting out a huge sigh each time he grew deeper and deeper inside of me. Sitting himself up more and back against the foot of his wood bed he pulled my body closed to his and began moving with me, slowly. Our movements were in sync and felt good, but enough of the love making crap. I pushed him away from my body with my right hand and took charge. Spreading my legs apart and planting my feet onto the bed I began to hump his dick. With quick, fast movements, not allowing my pussy to rest on his dick too long, I started closing my inner thighs each time I reached the top of his dick, causing my muscles to contract. He reached up to my neck with his left hand and tenderly began chocking me, man that turned me on. With his right hand he began rubbing the top of my hair, stroking it. Trying to maintain my movements I tuned out what he was doing and sat down on his dick really hard, forcing his dick to hit the base of my vagina. I pounced hard on his dick a good five more times before I couldn't take it anymore, I began to moan. He started shushing me, but it was too late. Between the noise from the bed and my moans, Chris had to have heard us. The next thing, all we hear is the door closing. DAYUM, he saw my ass. I didn't care if he heard us, but him seeing my ass was a different story. I quickly hopped up from his dick, grabbed my underwear and pants, hide on the side of the bed and slide my articles on clothing on.

I felt bad for leaving Craig just dick hanging all out like that but man, Chris could have had a camera taking pictures of my ass. I know I said I wanted them to have a story to talk about, didn't mean for it to be that detailed though.

Clit Chronicles: Something's Missing

My wife isn't able to complete me sexually, I really wish she were able to but there's always something missing. I enjoy making love to her but I'm never satisfied. I love my wife with my heart and soul so it's hard for me to come to grips with reality that I enjoy having sex with men. I don't believe that I am gay but the way I carry on is one of a gay man. I met Stephen about five months ago playing basketball at Chastain Memorial Park, here in Atlanta. It was my regular Saturday routine to ball with the guys, but it was my first time seeing Stephen. We exchanged very limited conversation our first meeting but by the second meeting I found out he was a Manager of some up and coming rap group and was looking for a Web Designer to create the group's web site; which I just so happen to be. I shot him my number and told him to call me Monday and he did. We had set up a time to meet at my office in Buckhead at 3:30 to go over what exactly he wanted the site to look like and pricing to do so. Somehow we got to talking about sports, our wives, our lives and everything else; conversation of web sites never came up. We shared a few drinks, watched some television talked some more and before we knew it the time had showed 9:00. My wife wasn't really one to check up on me but Stephen had it different in his house. His wife called a little after 9 asking where he was and what he was doing. I could hear her accusing him of cheating and everything else. He ended the phone call and looked stressed out, told me his wife was working his nerves and he couldn't take it anymore. He said he loved her but there was something missing. In the mist of just sitting on my leather couch in front of the television and him going on and on about his wife, I stopped him in his tracks and asked him if he had ever been with a man. I don't really know where that question came from because I had never been with a man or ever thought of being with one. I was just very comfortable with him and it was something different than the way I felt when I hung with my boys. I have friends from grade school I still chill with but I've never been able to listen and open up with them the way Stephen and I were. He seemed shocked and confused by my answer and started waving his hands around in the air saying he wasn't into that gay shit. I hadn't meant to offend him; it really was just a question. I apologized for making him uncomfortable and tried to change the subject back to basketball or anything. Out of the blue he asked me the same question and I told him no. There was an awkward silence for about five seconds and then he reached over with his right hand and grabbed my left leg.

Our eyes made contact and without further conversation we scooted closer to one another. Not talking about what was going on and just doing it made it not seem so bad and wrong. With him to my left and eyeing him, I began to unfasten my black slacks and gestured with my left hand for him to do the same. As he removed his jeans, I took my dick out of my boxers and began stroking it; Stephen joined in and jacking his dick off after removing his underwear. Don't ask me what we were doing on even what we were thinking but we just continued to beat our meat and then switched and allowed one another to satisfy the other. The small circle he made with his right index and thumb felt surreal going up and down the tip of my dick; my wife had never made hand pleasure feel this good.

Clit Chronicles: He's Magically Delicious

I woke up this morning with and my uvula was bothering me. For a moment I almost panicked thinking I may have strep throat but then the memories of last night came to mind; Markel played a game of tag with the back of my throat last night. A slight smile ran across my face as I rolled over to my right side in bed. Yeah, it's all coming back to me now, here is where he climbed inside my pussy with his huge dick making me wetter than ever. Running my left arm across the right side of the bed, the smell of his cologne hit my nose, smelling fresh as if he was still there and never left in the middle of the night. Markel had surprised me with a visit, I wasn't expecting him because I knew he had finals to study for. We had talked on the phone most of the night but little did I know he was driving to my house the whole time. When I heard the knock at the door I was taken a back by it; I was wearing my purple hair scarf, my white T. Mac shirt with holes in it and a pair of blue thongs. I wasn't expecting anyone so there was no way I was even going to the peep hole for the stranger to hear my footsteps. Markel started laughing as I was whispering to him that someone was at my door. "Open the door silly, its me." *Gasp* Dashing to the door I hurried and turned the locks; the dead bolts and chains were on. Once the door was open his fragrance hit me instantly; Unforgivable by Diddy. His big bright smile greeted me next; his teeth are so perfect. I jumped and gave him a huge hug, he stands 6'1 to my 5'5. Letting go of our embrace we walked into the living room and sat on the couch, me on the left side and him on the right. He closed in on me and gave me a kiss on the forehead, most women think the forehead kiss is non personal and dislike it, but his forehead kisses are so sweet and tender. I brought my right hand to the back of his neck and pulled him close to me, I was so happy to see him. With our faces close enough to kiss, I began to rub my nose up against his. Feeling like a little school girl, all giddy and happy, I climbed on top of him, startling him. He began to fondle and caress my breast with his right hand. His touch felt so good that I felt compelled to arch my back and sway back in forth. He took his left arm and supported my back as I let my body just flow with the touch of his hands across my body. His hand went from my breast to my neck, smoothly working his fingers up to my chin and finally sliding his index finger into my mouth. I began to suck on his finger, nibbled on it some and went back to sucking it. The teasing of his finger in my mouth only made me want to suck his dick and taste him.

Sitting back up, I began to unbutton his belt buckle and once that was undone I worked my way to his jeans and finally into his briefs, pulling out the treasure I was searching for. Feeling all excited like a Leprechaun, I slightly lifted up off of him, kneeling in between his legs, scooting him to the edge of the couch and sliding his pants down off his body. Gripping his dick with my left hand, I teased him a tad by simply licking the tip of his dick a few times and then finally quickly sliding it into my mouth. The moans that came from him let me know he was already loving it. Getting my mouth wet, I began to slurp his man hood, holding the shaft down with my right hand, shaking his dick inside my mouth, allowing it to hit the side walls of my mouth. Relaxing my muscles at the back of my throat I allowed his dick complete access to my mouth. Bobbing my head up and down, having his dick at the back of my mouth as he gripped my head, I started to work my throat muscles around his dick each time it hit my uvula. He began to grind his hips and move with me as I made love to him with my mouth. Taking his dick out of my mouth I began to stroke his shaft with my right hand, the wetness from my mouth made this technique very pleasurable. Spreading his legs apart some, I placed my head deep between his legs and allowed my mouth to meet with his balls. Placing one ball in my mouth at a time, as I continued to stroke him, he started running his fingers around my ears, pinching the tip of them and finally squeezing them; it was almost as if he was releasing that great pleasure through his fingers to my ears. Trying to keep things exciting I cupped both of his balls into my mouth and started humming, the trembling from my mouth onto his nut sack produced a great sensation. Peeking up at him, he had his eyes closed and was moaning louder and louder.   After a few moments of humming on his balls, I put his dick back into my mouth and he stood up. Scooting further back from the couch on my knees, I welcomed him and his new position; opening my mouth wider, using my tongue to twirl around the head of his penis and then quickly intaking it inside my mouth. Each time that I slide his dick into my mouth, I squeezed my cheeks together making my mouth a replica of my pussy; tight and wet. I knew that the position I was in now would allow me to suck his dick until he came. With a few pelvic thrust he let me know that him reaching that point was near and he wanted to end it with a bang. Letting the back of my mouth expand, as I kept my lips pressed close together, I gave him the okay to violate my mouth

violently with his dick. He rammed his dick so far into my mouth I began to gag, choke, drool and tear up. That didn't stop me from what I was doing, my mission was to make him cum. Even though I was gagging it wasn't bad; I could handle it. He took his right hand, took a hand full of my hair, pushed the top of my head down and continued ramming all 9.5 inches into my mouth. I felt him hit the back of my throat countless times, it was something that I had NEVER experienced. He then took his left hand and began jacking the base of his dick; he was cumming. Still gripping my hair, he tilted my head back some, pulling my mouth slightly away from his dick, and continued to beat his meat. Stroking it all the way to the tip, his natural flavors of body fluids squirted into my mouth. When I felt he had his final drop out, I slide his dick back into my mouth, sucking the tip real hard and swallowed the tip. Even though I allowed my muscles to go through the motions of swallowing, I didn't exactly swallow his juices; I had been choking and gagging so much I feared I'd throw up if I swallowed his continents. I hope he didn't take my spitting his nut out as a bad sign. The flavor that I was able to savor in my mouth was delightful. I look forward to the next time I'm able to really satisfy him completely.

I knew he had to get back to studying, so him leaving didn't bother me. Maybe next trip I'll get lucky and actually have him hold me all night.

Clit Chronicles: Time For Excitement

I was in the mood for something different this time around. You've pleased each and every time I'm with you and I want to return the favor with a little excitement. The knock at the door startled you some; you didn't know I was expecting company. In walks a light skinned, slim but thick chick with a huge grin on her face and she's looking as if she's ready to get down to business. Taking my hand and walking me to the couch next to you, she slides off my blue shorts and underwear, lays me on the couch, takes her pants off and underwear, then places her head between my legs. She toots her naked ass in the air, not too far from your face; an invitation for you to go for it. Hiding your head in her airborne pussy, you take your right hand and begin to separate her pussy lips. She gets crazy with the head she's giving me, starts moving her head really fast right to left, left to right, waggling her butt as she's moving. I pull her head up and motion 4 her to help me with you, she gets down on her knees in front of you, unbuttons your pants and pulls your dick out. I stand on top of the couch, stand over you with my pussy in your face, tilt your head back and straddle your face. You lift your right hand and start palming my ass, pushing me down closer to your face. She's still down there giving you head, deep throat-ing your huge dick - I wonder if she is enjoying your flavor as much as I do. The moans coming from her as she's stroking, licking and sucking the tip of your dick assures me she loves pleasing you just as much as I do. Still straddled upon your face, I begin to grind my hips on your face as you slide your tongue inside of me allowing my sweet warm juices to fill your mouth.   We kept at this position for five more minutes, her sucking you and you licking me, until you felt it was time for a change. Slowly lifting me up off of your face and sliding your dick out of her mouth, you tell me to lay on the couch on the right and for her to lay on the left side. You straddling my mouth, sliding your dick in my mouth and as you began sucking my clit upside down. You don't want to leave Light Bright hanging so you slide two fingers in her pussy and start finger fucking her. Covering my pussy up with your mouth, you start nibbling and sucking my clit as your dick is in my mouth throbbing and growing. Your sweet juices flowing from the tip of your dick into my mouth; I love it. You grinding your hips and riding my face as you continue to keep your face buried in my pussy; lets stay n this position until we cum together. The finger session Light Bright is getting must be a good one; her moans are so loud its causing me to moan. The two of us moaning together turns you on, lifting your head from between my legs you tell us you're about to cum and you want us both to taste it. Getting up for the position you are in, you stand and start stroking your dick. Motioning for us to get down in front of you, your strokes become more intense. As we comply and kneel down in front of you, you slightly bend your knees and hold your dick at an angle. Jerking your dick and swaying it from side to side, within three minutes mine and Light Bright's faces were covered with your semen. Looking at one another and without thought, she and I began kissing, smearing your love even deeper into our faces. How's that for excitement?

Clit Chronicles: Oh No He Didn't

Something told me not to go into the city last night. If I hadn't gone, then I wouldn't be in the mess I'm in now. No, I take that back. Drinking that last bit of Hypnotiq wouldn't have made me open my mouth the way I did, but that one shot of Hennessey I drank after last call! Well, let's just say that was all I needed to act like a fool, and God knows I did. But I don't take all the blame for what happened though. Kenny knew that just by him bringing that white girl into the Dew Drop Inn with him, that he was pushing the limits of my patience. The minute I saw her on his arm; sauntering around like she was some damn body; I knew that him toting that blonde haired bitch around was his stab at getting back at me. It was going to be just a matter of time before I was going to have to give him and that stringy haired wench a solid piece of my mind. Hell, when all was said and done...he was lucky her jaw was all the hell I broke up in there! Three weeks ago I was the chick on Kenny's arm – one year and a half of my life thrown out the window after one night of giving the man I love his fantasy with Bambi. That's what I'm calling the tramp, Bambi; she doesn't deserve the respect to be called by her real name, Cindy. Kenny threw hints at me about having a 3sum with him and a chick; I should have known he and the white bimbo had something going on because the instant I said, "Okay", she was at my house the next day ready for action. She wore a red tight fitted mini dress with red pumps, walking behind Kenny as he walked in the door. I did a double take and asked him what was going on and he said "Today is the day. This is Cindy and she's here to join us." Join us?! What the hell? Ok calm down, Kim. I got up and walked into the kitchen and poured myself a glass of red wine as they sat on the couch whispering something amongst them. I walked back into the living room and then made a right and found myself into the bedroom. I sat in the dark room on the edge of the bed for about two minutes before Kenny came in after me. He never said a word, just started kissing me, touching my breast and caressing me. I allowed myself to let loose, drop my head back and finally allowing my shoulders to hit the bed. His kisses made their way from my lips, to my neck, to my breast, stomach and finally around my hips. Kenny began unzipping my pants and finally pulling them down along with my panties. The next thing I felt were his lips around my throbbing clit. He had never sucked it so good before, it felt so good my body started moving on it's on. His tongue flickered really fast onto my clit before he gave it one big lick and finally sucking the outside of my lips. He worked his way inside my opening and licking my inner walls, while his lips covered my lips. He took his right hand, pressed my lips apart with thumb and index finger and got sloppy mc-nasty with it; his salvia mixed with my juices. I reached out with my right hand to the top of his head to press it closer into me. Okay, this is NOT the top of my man's head; looking down I see Cindy going to town on my treasure like she was a

fat black man on New Years Eve eating Chitterlings. Oh Snap! It felt too good to make her stop, but I wanted her to stop – I think. Dropping my head back onto the bed and raising my right leg onto the bed I just enjoyed the moment. She knew what she was going and I didn't want to stop her. The next thing I know, I felt her face banging into me. What Now?!!? I looked up and saw Kenny standing behind Cindy, as she was on her knees, giving her the business with Slugger. She was sticking her butt out and in the air so he could get in better, but he still had to get up under her in a slight angle to get it how he wanted it. He was ramming his stuff inside of her so hard and fast that it slipped out and landed on the top of her butt. Looking at his long, thick pole, I began to get more wet and excited – his manhood does something to me. But then I noticed it wasn't covered with any protection; what the hell? I jumped up so fast, scooted back on the bed and began yelling. No this fool was not hunching some chick and wasn't wrapped up!! I looked at him and he asked me, "What's wrong, Babe? You want to feel me inside you now?" Is this man mental? "No you moron!! And why are you not strapped up? You're sleeping with some unknown chick, increasing the chance of me receiving an STD, are you crazy?!?" I guess Bambi got offended by my rant, she sucked her teeth but she fixed that real fast when I gave her a "Trick don't go there" look. I yelled for about 5 more minutes about how trifling Kenny was and told him to get the pink toe out of my house and for him to tag along with her. Well, that's what he did and found his clothes on the lawn the next day with locks changed. Three weeks later he was walking in Dew Drop Inn with the same skank and I just lost it. She looked at me and that's all it took for me to get up to them, stand in front of her and punched her in her grill. It all happened so fast, I looked up and saw her on the ground covering her mouth. Again, they are both lucky her jaw was the only thing broke up in that piece!

Clit Chronicles: I'm his Whore

Never in all of my life have I met a man that complete me to the level where I feel I want to be his, how do I say, ummm slut!! It's something about the way he makes me feel; comfortable and free, that inhibits me to do any and everything to please him to the best of my ability. I'm talking that Janet Jackson, Any Time Any Place type sex with a touch of Adina Howard Freak In Me!!

I met Andre about three months ago but the way we've been hanging, fucking, sucking and licking, you'd swear it's been three years. It takes time to get to a level with someone where you feel relaxed to do certain things, things you've never tried and so on, things a man would want his wife to do; all men want their wives to be their slut, whore. We've grown close to one another and have done things people in relationships do and I trust him because he's down for me as I am for him. There was the time at the movies we sat in the middle row; the place was pretty packed, not full to capacity but full enough. Andre sat to the right of me in the theatre, we had only been there for about 20 minutes before I reached over with my left hand and started massaging his dick through his jeans; gripping it from its base to the tip, applying pressure as I got closer to his tip. Feeling his dick grow always turned me on. I could tell he was a tad shy because of all the people around us but I didn't give a fuck!! With my right hand I proceeded to unzip his jeans, kept doing that without stopping the flow of stroking his dick with my left hand. With his zipper down and his curved dick laying on his right thigh, I slid my left hand inside his Tommy Hilfiger boxers and fondled around until I was able to lay eyes on his huge, black, enormous, gargantuan, massive cock; my treat!! Getting my mouth watered up with saliva, I hunched over closer to his dick and welcomed up inside my hot, warm, tight, juicy mouth; home. My plan was to tease him just a taste before I really went to work on MY dick. His body began shifting around so I peeked up at him, expecting him to be in heaven but instead he was looking around to see if anyone saw what I was doing. I'm a cocky bitch, I need all attention on me and my pleasing him so I put my head back down and took his dick in my mouth like a popsicle, lifting my tongue up as if a doctor were checking my throat and sliding it out of a small opening of my mouth to reach his balls and cupping them with my tongue all at once. I felt his body jerk, that's when I knew I had his attention. Not stopping the moment, I opened my mouth wider and found my way back to the tip of his dick and back to the base, allowing his dick to reach the back of my throat hitting my vocal cords.

Sucking his dick was all good and dandy, but I wanted to feel him in my pussy. Since we went together and got tested for all STI's and I got on the pill, his dick has made a home in my pussy. I wish I were wearing a skirt because it would have been easier access, but fuck it!! Lifting myself up from his lower half I quickly undid my pants and slid them down to my ankles, stepping out of them with my left leg. I was trying not to bring too much attention to us but I heard the lady behind me suck her teeth as if to say, "Oh no she didn't" I turned around, looked at her and her man; shot her a look as to say, "Bitch you need to be doing this to your man!!" Andre sat there in disbelief but didn't dare stop me as I straddled him backwards, pulled my thong to the side and welcomed him into my cave. Gripping the seat in front on me and arching my back and spreading my legs open more; I bounced up and down on his dick like a pogo stick. I felt his dick deep inside of me as he took a hold of my ass cheeks and gripped the bottom of it; giving me more leverage and assisting me with my bouncing. My pussy got so wet so fast; his curved dick hit spots I didn't know I had. I tightened my pussy around his dick each time I went to the top of it, only to have my pussy throb like a heart beat as I slowly made my way to the base of his dick. I knew neither of us would be getting a nut, we had drew too much attention to ourselves with our grunting and moaning, but damn it sure felt good. Of course we were escorted out of the movie theatre but it was well worth it. Oh and then there was another unforgettable experience at his Cousins house. We stopped by just to hang out, no more than six people at the crib watching television or playing PS3. For some reason, when Andre was playing PS3, the frustration he displayed while losing got me wet; I wanted him to take his frustration out on my pussy. My pussy lips were whispering his name. I excused myself to the bathroom after he finished his game, sat on the toilet and texted him asking him to join me in the bathroom. As soon as he walked in the door I pushed him up against the wall, kissed him roughly as I unzipped his pants, slide down to my knees and happily accepted his dick inside my saturated mouth. Just wanting to get his dick wet I allowed him to fuck my mouth a good 10 strokes, I could tell by the way he gripped my hair and pulled my face closer to his privates that he was enjoying that shit. I took my right hand and started stroking his dick as he continued to fuck my face. With his dick wet just the way I wanted it and him still against the wall, I pulled my jeans down and bent over in front of him and slide his dick in my pussy. I felt like Tigger from Winnie the Pooh as I sprung up and down on his dick with my rear. Wanting to feel him deeper inside of me, I bent over as far as I could and gripped the bank of my ankles, spreading my legs open further and giving him a better opening to my pussy. The way his penis eased in and out, deep and strong, moving inside of my wetness I couldn't help but scream, "DADDY". I could tell he was in an ecstatic delight of great pleasure, elation and joy when I said that; he took his left hand and began slapping my ass like I were a bad girl in school. He mumbled he was about to come; I wanted to taste his sweet nut so I quickly turned around and got on my knees, gripped the tip of his dick with my right hand and stroked it while sucking the tip as I worked my way down. Within seconds I was gargling his nut like it was mouthwash; protein

does a body good!! I was about to swallow but wanted him to feel my gulp, so I pressed my lips to his tip, sucking it real tight, then swallowing; savoring its taste in one huge gulp. Women these days need to stop being scared to please the man they are with. Be that slut, whore, bitch or whatever. You can't be that way with everyone though, you'll know if you've got the man you're intended to do those things with once you feel he appreciates the pleasure you give him. You can see it in his eyes and hear it in his voice. Don't be afraid to let that man choke you a bit or bite your nipples; let him be Tarzan and you his Jane.

Clit Chronicles: Mr Man & His Dong

Not one of my usual stories; left ya hanging a tad :) but you get the drift of things!! I recently learned that size does matter, lol, and wanted to write a tale about it, lol!! But I'm hungry so I ended up cutting it short to go get food - and YES, I mean FOOD!!! The blood vessels in my pussy are in love with the substantial amount of Dong "Mr. Man" is blessed with; she gets VERY wet. The moistness of my pussy allows him to bathe inside of me forever. The pleasure his penis brings my honey pot is mind blowing and everlasting pleasure! Not only did he make me cream and bring me to ecstasy he did it two times and left me dripping down my left thigh. He left me unable to walk without shivering or trembling. My pussy was far from parched after a night with "Mr Man" and the thrusting of his pelvis pushing his dick deep inside of me had me calling him, "Daddy" and wanting more.

I was never one who believed sized mattered or even that all tall men were blessed; to be honest I never cared about the size of a dick just as long as I got penetration!! I met "Mr. Man" one night at the club, a night where I just happened to be "the shit in that muthafucka" cause men on top of men were trying to get my number. I held conversations with a few of them following that night, but there was something about the sincerity of his voice and de-meanor that attracted me to him. I wasn't sure what he was about but I saw nothing wrong with spending time with him and seeing exactly he had to offer - friendship wise of course. He picked me up from my apartment and I must say, I was not disappointed with the first impression. The conversation while riding to his house was intriguing and relaxing, I felt comfortable with opening up to him as a friend but felt potential to open up more as a lov-er. The day was a blast, laughs and smiles all day. He even showed me his cooking skills magic and made me a steak dinner; did I mention the man is 6'5, 255? I didn't want the day to end but I was raised old school and that spending time with a man beyond the hours of 10pm was nothing more than booty call hours, also that sleeping with a man on the first night was a no-no!! Again, I didn't want the night to end and he showed respect for me throughout the day, I saw no reason to feel I'd be uncomfortable with him if I stayed longer.

We watched movies, shared laughs and witty conversation until the late hours of the night. It must have been the ending of "Waist Deep" that had me all soft and wanting affection - watching Tyrese appear from the "dead" to join his girl and son left me all warm and emotional inside - I scooted closer to "Mr Man" on the love seat and gave the notion that I wanted more personal attention from him. Sitting to the left of me he wrapped his right arm around my shoulders and pulled me closer to his solid body. Looking up into his eyes, I moved in and blessed him with a kiss; his lips are so full and tender, soft yet firm. That was the moment I knew I wanted to share my Pom Pom with him. Moving our bodies closer together he picked me up from the love seat, carried me upstairs to his king sized bed and laid me on his purple bed spread (he's a Que). He looked me in the eyes and asked me if I was sure about taking it to the next level. I answered him by pulling his body closer to me and kissing those tender lips again. The murmurs coming from my body became intense and deep, I had to have him now. Unbuttoning my jeans and raising my black top, he fondled around with my breast and expressed his desire to tease me before pleasing me. Reaching down to his waist I wanted to touch what he had in his jeans, I underestimated him completely, I was not expecting him to he so hung. Not only was he hung but he was thick and full; I don't think I can handle him. Never underestimate the power of a skinny bitch with a deep pussy and passion for a man with a enormous peter!!

www.ingramcontent.com/pod-product-compliance
Lightning Source LLC
Chambersburg PA
CBHW071223170626
46809CB00005BA/1911